THE ILLUSION OF *Love*

NAVNIT SINGH

The Illusion of Love
Copyright © 2022 by Navnit Singh

All rights reserved. No part of this
publication may be reproduced, distributed,
or transmitted in any form or by any means,
including photocopying, recording, or
other electronic or mechanical methods,
without the prior written permission of
the author, except in the case of brief
quotations embodied in critical reviews
and certain other non-commercial
uses permitted by copyright law.

Tellwell Talent
www.tellwell.ca

ISBN
978-0-2288-8377-7 (Hardcover)
978-0-2288-8376-0 (Paperback)
978-0-2288-8378-4 (eBook)

To my family:

My mom, my dad, Harjot,
Jas and my dog, Kami.

To Captain H. Bal., After my Dad passed
away, he treated me like his own child.

To Raman, who is the sister I never had.

To my best friends, Sana and Bethany.

And finally, to all my beloved cousins,
aunts, uncles and grandparents.

Table of Contents

LUST 1

Enticing Poison 3

Enchanted Fantasy 5

A Thousand Years 7

Painful Pleasure 9

The Unknown 10

Endless Thoughts 13

Beloved Desire 15

Picture Perfect 17

Abyss 19

LOVE 21

Thank You 22

You Bring Me Back 25

Tough Love 27

Self-Love 29

Mama Bear 31

Nature's Beauty 32

Glad I Gave You a Shot 34

Finish the Race. 37

My Other Half 39

Tri-Coloured Beauty. 41

Start Over 42

My Precious Treasure 44

Lessons Learned from Sloppy Kisses 47

Spirited Nature. 49

Lean on Me 51

Cookie 53

Crumble 55

LIES **57**

Immune 59

Angel 61

Deceit. 63

Hut 65

Last Resort 66

Confined 69

Wanderer. 71

Broken Dreams/
Green-Eyed Monster (Part 1) 72

Broken Dreams/
Green-Eyed Monster (Part 2) 74

Stay 77

Over 79

Took 81

LOSS **83**

Eyes 85

Fire 87

Demons Beware 88

Perfect Motion 91

Flip Side 93

Realization 95

Treasure 97

You Do You; I'll Do Me 99

Strange Footsteps 101

Empty Space 103

Hidden Feelings 105

Uneasy Slumber 107

Lost Cause	109
Fate's Fortune	110
Silent Symphony	113
Judge a Book	115
Pain	117
Mourn	119
When	121
Red Sky	123
Thorns	125
Heart	127
Stained Petals	128
Veins	131
Soul	133
In Love	135
Story of My Life	137

LUST

Enticing Poison

I long to be stripped
Of the desire
To taste your sweet poison,
For when my urges
Are quenched,
Soon after,
The temptation
That drives me crazy
Only doubles in size.

Enchanted Fantasy

Emerged under the sea,
Soaring through the clouds,
Leaping over skyscrapers,
Blending into the scene,
A place where anything is possible,
As long as you believe.
Extraordinary things go unquestioned,
Dreaming as if you live forever,
Imagination running wild and free,
No care in the world,
Without a thought,
Revealing your heart's true desires.
No doubt
Watching events from your day,
Repeating like it's on replay,
Filled with happiness and hope,
It will surely begin.
Just turn off the lights,
With a pillow or two,
And close your eyes.

A Thousand Years

Never have I ever encountered such a beautiful mystery before. With long, bouncy curls, rosy cheeks and eyes that make it seem like she has seen it all, her mascara-filled lashes have the ability to bat away any hesitations. Could she be the one? Her beckoning grin makes my pounding heart practically leap out of my chest. Daringly, I edge a little closer for I want nothing more than to bask in her brilliance. Steadily, I close the distance between us. I feel our fates have intertwined from the moment our eyes first met. The angelic aura illuminating off her is intoxicatingly enjoyable. To spend a thousand years by her side would never suffice the hunger burning deep in my very soul.

Painful Pleasure

Breathe it in;
Let it consume you.
Sweet, seductive fragrances
Seeping from within,
Attracting many.
Heads turning,
All in awe,
Vivid sensation,
Distorted thoughts,
Joyous pleasure,
Grasping the forbidden fruit
In the palm of your hand.
Thorns like daggers
Submerging eagerly into your flesh,
Tearing the soft seal of protection above,
Dripping the warmth hidden within
Flowing through your veins,
Left in soreness and disarray,
Soaked in a sea of red.

The Unknown

Curiosity takes off,
Mischief running wild,
Pondering deep in awe,
Wondering where such beauty
Was hidden away from me for so long.
I cannot seem to take my eyes off of her.
Everything about her is just so magical.
How I long to touch her luscious bouncy curls.
I'm tempted to do just that, and so,
With the dark goddess staring back at me,
Showing no obvious signs of objection,
I reach out to touch
The mysterious masterpiece before me,
Only to have my hand slapped away
By dear Mother.
Oh, how kind Mother is to me.
She must have saved me from the unknown,
For only she knows what is best for me.
And so, for now,
I will sit quietly on the bus and obey
As we wait for our stop to arrive.

Glad I did not get contaminated;
For all I know it was mud on her skin.
Note to self: never try to ask, touch or talk to
The unknown, ever again.
And so, yet another successful lesson learned.
So happy I have my mother's example
To follow in her footsteps
And obey her every instruction.
Only then will I hopefully be given the chance
To pass down what I learned:
Leave the unknown unexplored.

Endless Thoughts

It's as if she teleported out of thin air.
One moment no one's there,
And the next, she appears.

See, I have a theory
That people seem to sneak up on you
If you're not paying attention.
At times you may think your vulnerability increases,
Like when you puncture your toe,
You find yourself staggering about.

As the girl takes long strides towards you,
You snap out of your pondering.
Now that you have a better look,
You realize it's your tutor.

As you mumble a hello,
She entangles her hand in her hair.
Both of you are passive.

The conversation ends as quickly as it began.

Beloved Desire

I attempt to steer clear;
However, your secret weapon is unleashed:
Deliciously-laced kisses
And a deep aftertaste.
As logic leaves my body,
My mind is filled with you.
Before I know it,
I'm engulfed
In your everlasting abyss.

Picture Perfect

Maybe the people
Who are far away
Only appear to be perfect
Because we have never
Seen them up close
And personal.

Abyss

You pulled me out
Of my own personal abyss,
Showing me love
I would have otherwise missed.

Thank You

Thank you for all that you do.
Without you,
I couldn't-wouldn't
Be able to stand on my own two feet.
From helping us stay nice and warm
To showing us how to beat the heat,
Sending endless gratitude
For your wonderful presence
And delightful attitude.
Providing smiles and laughter
Never looked so easy.
Neither did chowing down
On delicious food
Freshly prepared at home
With love in every bite.
With you there isn't any need to frown.
Your wisdom and strength
Guide us through the darkest of times,
Bringing light and a ray of hope
To a new beginning.
You helped us become who we are

Though friends influence
The direction of our footprints at times,
The soil in which they are made
Are forever unchanged,
Created by you and others.
Without a doubt, you are simply the best.
Forever grateful for everything.

You Bring Me Back

At times,
I wish my memory were vastly improved
In order to recite every word you speak.
For when times are tough,
It's very numbing and rough.
When others can't reach me
At the depths of an endless sea,
Your words speak to my very being,
Bringing a new ray of light within,
And awakening me.

Tough Love

Despite the violent swearing
And cold heart on display
That makes it all look so uncaring
Which results in my dismay,

I know you love and care
Deep down inside
Because you're always there
When I'm faced with a low tide.

I just wish we could assemble
In good times and in bad
Without me having to tremble
Or you blowing a gasket and getting really mad.

Maybe if you gain more tolerance
And I become a little more mature,
We can have lots of fun together,
Building something we can both finally endure.

Self-Love

Paint your own canvas
Any which way you want,
Whether it be your face, hair or clothes,
And truly don't care
What they think.
It's all about how you feel.
See, trying to fit into society's norms
Can bring a great deal of anxiety.
So be free to fill your own life's masterpiece
With any colour, brush, material or technique,
And don't worry about going out of the lines,
Because it just adds to the authenticity
Of your work,
Making it something to look back on
And be proud of.

Mama Bear

You sound like my mother,
And you look like her too.
Giving caring advice
Along with words of wisdom,
Always making sure
I eat my fill and I'm bundled up.
Kind, loving
And full of intuition,
A mother is a mother,
Whether she's a mother
To a duck
Or to a bear.

Nature's Beauty

He is like the landscape,
Reliable and strong.
Always there,
Rain or shine,
Chiselled to perfection.
He is the foundation
I walk along.

His voice is like the river,
Soothing and yet uneven,
So calming to hear,
Bringing peace within,
Or, if need be,
Raging and loud.

His spirit is like the sun,
Warm and bright,
Turning my frowns
The other way around
And shining
Ever so brilliantly.

His intent is like the moonlight,
Pure yet mysterious.
Innocently out and about
While what he wants
Remains a question,
But alas a mystery
I intend to solve.

Glad I Gave You a Shot

The very thought of you brings great joy to me.
You're such a true friend.
So, by your side, I will be.
I know we can make it to the end.

We have honestly come a long way
From playing on opposing teams
And not listening to a word the other had to say,
Never thinking we would one day be confined
in our dreams.

I thought I saw some good within;
Thus, I tried to get to know you more
Only to discover my best friend
Without having my face slammed in any doors.

Once we were more or less on the same page,
I believe that's when we grew
To the point where we had truly entered a
golden age
Where you are now a part of the trusted few.

With you, there's no need to be blue.
The comforting words you speak
Make it look like my smile was put in place with glue!
Now excuse me while I go rub my cheeks.

Finish the Race

Keep your head held high
For you're almost at the finish line.
You've done this before
And I know you can do it again.
All you have to do is believe
In a better tomorrow
And not fill yourself with any more sorrow.
So, dry up those tears;
Now's a time to be headstrong.
Go exterminate your fears.

My Other Half

You truly are my other half;
I don't care what people think.
With you, I can sincerely laugh
And that's just with a little wink.

You always know how to make me happy
Or when something's wrong.
Who cares if I'm getting sappy;
I want to be with you lifelong.

Although there are some rough patches
Here and there, or a little long-distance issue,
We always make it without any scratches.
So hey, at least we won't need a tissue!

I guess it's because we're pact sisters
Through and through.
Together we can be two terrifying twisters;
It's no wonder the rest have a lot to live up to!

Tri-Coloured Beauty

Your tiny wagging tail
Greets me feverishly at the door.
As we exchange our eager hellos,
You give out ticklish kisses
That have patiently waited
For my very arrival.
I present you yet another squeaky toy
That hastily makes its way into your mouth.
An enlightening series of games follows
And before we know it,
We're huddled up by the couch
With your muzzle buried in my lap;
Time for a nap.

Start Over

You may not be able
To completely understand me,
And I, you,
But I'm sure our feelings
When expressed
Reach each other,
And that itself is more than enough.
At times I may not have the best mindset
In the world,
But I have come to realize
I need to pull myself together
For your sake,
As well as my own.
I would ask
To be forgiven,
But I know you don't hold anything
Against me.

So, if possible,
Let's simply put an end
To these bad vibes
And begin anew,
Filled with adventures, laughter, hope,
But above all: love.

My Precious Treasure

He's as agile
As his heart is fragile
And at the top of his class
With a little bit of sass.

He loves anything athletic
Because he's so energetic
And his favourite kind of deals
Are the ones that end with meals.

He shows so much loyalty
As if we are royalty.
He's always on guard,
Making falling asleep anything but hard.

It's so horrible
How he's so adorable,
You'll want to snuggle with him
Simply based on a whim.

But the best part
Is that he stole my heart,
So, if he ever needs me in his endeavours,
I'll always be there for him forever.

Lessons Learned from Sloppy Kisses

Be courageous for yourself and others,
Love with all your heart,
Be thankful for every meal received,
Listen to your parents,
Greet family with open arms,
Forgive and forget,
Get off the couch and move,
Make new friends wherever you go,
Always be on your best behaviour,
Go outside and enjoy the breeze,
Take it easy when you're tired,
And it's always the perfect time
For hugs and kisses.

Spirited Nature

He's one quiet mouse
Who's as cunning as a fox.
Like a hungry hippo
With the hyperactiveness of a squirrel.
He has his moments
When he's a mischievous monkey
Due to his inner playful seal.
But who can resist his dashing looks
That qualify him to be
More elegant than a songbird,
With the ideals of a noble steed.
Protection is no question
Due to his honourable wolf roots
Allied with his lionheartedness,
And, through it all,
He's my little lamb who follows me everywhere,
But that's okay because
He's as cute as a panda,
Who's willing to be a cuddly teddy bear
When it's time to shut my tired eyes.
And I wouldn't have it
Any other way.

Lean on Me

We get along just dandy,
Without bribes made with any candy.
It's no wonder some say we get along;
You can usually find us listening to the same song.

We know how to make the other smile
Just with a simple idea or greeting.
Any amount of time spent is worthwhile,
And we never give each other a beating.

We have ridiculous nicknames
Accompanied with the silliest grins.
We always verse in games.
At heart, I'd say we're twins.

Cookie

You take care of everyone's needs
Except for your own
No matter what.
If you were a cookie,
You would offer everyone a bite,
Pretending you're fine,
Until you were reduced to crumbles.

Crumble

Asking for a break,
Her body lies still
While her world
Begins to disintegrate.

LIES

Immune

We become our own personal monsters
When we no longer flinch
At the sight of what
We once deemed despicable.

Angel

You were nothing but
An angel.
It was I
Who painted you out
To be the villain.

Deceit

How amusing it must be
For onlookers.
We claim to flourish
In each other's company
And long to be together,
Yet we take
The very first opportunity
We can snatch
To flee
From the other's clutches.

Hut

Maybe my best
Just wasn't enough
For you to stay.
Maybe, just maybe,
My little hut
Could have never been
Our home,
For my love is like
An inferno,
And yours
Is a measly spark.

Last Resort

No more telling lies;
I've finally decided
To cut all ties.
As much as I tried,
I see you couldn't care less.
Ignoring me and never willingly being there
Resulted in me becoming one big mess,
Attempting to piece myself together,
Just ending up with lots of stress.

I didn't want to confess.
Maybe it's meant to be,
Because this can't be solved with a measly hug.
At a time long before,
You were a beloved part of me.
But now you're just an addiction,
Causing endless pain
Wishing you'd pay attention.

Not only do I feel we drifted,
But we barely have anything in common,
Leaving our goals and dreams heavily conflicted.
Maybe it's from our different lifestyles,
Or the influence of friends.
Still, it's no excuse
For the sorrow
That resonates within me.
And for these reasons,
I'm cutting you off for good,
Because, you see,
This isn't just the changing of seasons.

Confined

Shoving nonsense
Down my throat
In an effort
To rescue me,
Thinking you know better.
My opinions fall
On deaf ears,
Forced to listen
And carry on
With your way of thinking.
Your beliefs clash with mine.
But I am not to make a peep.
For what do I know?
You say you know me
Better than I
Know myself.

Wanderer

I would say I lost you
After you were found,
But a wanderer
Could never be held bound.

Broken Dreams/Green-Eyed Monster (Part 1)

After pouring enormous amounts
Of time and all my energy
Into this sport of mine,
I feel it slowly become a part of me.
It's my life.
After working tirelessly,
My efforts will be paid off.
I can see it now:
They will announce the award
Accompanied by my glorious name.
Finally, I will receive the recognition I deserve.

The award is given
To me;
It is not.
What is rightfully mine
Is taken away from me,
Not only robbed outright,
But given to my so-called best friend.
Why must she steal all my life's achievements?

My happiness?
What's the point if I always fall short of first place
When it comes to her?
I swear
To never try again.

Broken Dreams/Green-Eyed Monster (Part 2)

After putting it all on the line
And giving it my all and then some,
I know I tried my best
And that's all that matters.
I will happily cheer on my beloved bestie.
If she were to win,
Even if it means I didn't,
I know we both worked vigorously
And stayed strong until the end.
We did great, my friend.
I wish her nothing but the best in the world.
I would love nothing more
Than to see a smile simmering on her beautiful face.
I promise to be an endless supply
Of compliments!

As the award is being called
Our hearts skip a beat.
My name is called!
Overwhelming gratitude washes over me
And I'm the happiest girl in the entire room.
As I glance at my best friend,
Guilt consumes me.
I see nothing but the green-eyed monster
Staring back at me.
I ask you what's wrong,
But you say it's nothing.
Why can't you be happy for me
Just this once?
We're supposed to lift
Each other's spirits up,
Not send them crashing down.

Stay

No, he didn't tell me
Why he didn't stay,
But the way he left
Said more than he could ever say.

Over

The conversation
Ended abruptly
When she told him
To stop telling lies.

Took

You came
And you took,
And you took,
And you took.
Until I had nothing left to give.
So, in return you thanked me
With a revolting look.

Loss

Eyes

How can I see the light
Through closed eyes?

Pry them open.

Fire

If only my fire for you
Were extinguished,
Just like how your desire for me
Is now relinquished.

Demons Beware

He's a savage beast with a short temper and a devilish mindset. In order to have a brief glimpse at a tiny piece of his humanity the size of a pea, many horrible, twisted layers must be unearthed before his diabolical self manages to rear its ugly head once more. He naturally radiates a sinister aura, more wicked than any villain before him. He abuses young, defenceless beings who are unable to even utter a single word. Such rage and power aren't even shown to those who rival his strength. So why must he demonstrate such brutality and monstrous fury to the ones he claims to love and vowed to protect? We try to save the infant from harm's way when she mingles with peers, but even they wouldn't dare attack her the way he does once he unleashes his tremendous wrath time and time again. The one that should be restrained and distanced from the precious adopted child is the abomination that knows better but chooses to do worse. He brushes off warnings from onlookers. The mentality with this fiend is the innocent's blood shed for his accidental pain. The worst part is that this will continue long after his fragile punching bag is beaten, battered and bruised. His barbaric excuse for crippling her? She had it coming.

Perfect Motion

How could you get up and go
When everything
Was set in perfect motion
With you as my land,
And I
Your ocean?

Flip Side

    -rtive   -ll   -nto   swing.
Suppo-   friends pu- you o-   a
    -sed   -sh   -ff   bridge.

Realization

I'm not your
Go-to person,
Your priority,
Or entrusted
As your secret-keeper,
And I'm starting to learn
That's okay.

Treasure

My heart was a treasure
No one could uncover,
Until you took me on a date,
Only to discover,
I was far from your first mate.
Why,
I couldn't even be deemed your lover.

You Do You; I'll Do Me

The slightest high or low
Causes the biggest panics amongst them.
An emotionless doll,
Whose expression can be painted,
I am not.
So why must you insist
I act a certain way,
Putting on a pretty face
For the world to see
Even though it's eating away at me?
Please, just let me be.

Strange Footsteps

Your face resembles
That of a dear friend,
But your footsteps
Are that of a stranger.

Empty Space

It troubles me
How our severed bond
Doesn't faze you
In the slightest.

Maybe it's because
You found pieces
To fill the void,

While mine slowly
Turned into a black hole.

Hidden Feelings

Trying to pretend
That I don't care
About you
Is like trying to
Put out a house fire
With a torch.

Everything gets consumed
In your everloving flames.

Uneasy Slumber

The nights my head
Doesn't rest on your chest
Are the very nights
Unpleasant dreams await me.

Lost Cause

Switching effortlessly
From sweet and loving
To vicious and menacing
With dagger-like words
That pierce your crumbling shield,
Your thoughtful attempts to rescue me
Backfire and go unnoticed.
As a last resort,
You backpaddle out
The broken mansion engulfed in flames,
Without so much as a second glance.
And thus, another shattered relationship
Gradually fades into the distance
While I frantically
Try to mend
What fell apart,
Or worse:
What never was.

Fate's Fortune

A tragic end, just like a miscarriage,
So helpless and restrained,
No one going head over heels
Or finding true love.
Parents seal the deal;
You merely accept.
Treated as an unfeeling trophy
Simply auctioned away,
Dressed in the finest of clothes,
So shiny and new,
Very appealing,
And yet sold away
Without much to say.
Given away to the highest bidder,
Not knowing who they truly are:
A pure soul or a filthy one.
No idea how you'll be treated:
Kept nicely and neatly in the cabinet,
Or in the corner,
Covered in cobwebs.

With no clue as to what their real personality is:
Stubborn, selfish, sexist, ignorant, insane?
And yet you're expected to paint a smile on
And simply agree,
Or not at all, it doesn't matter
In the eyes of your parents,
Just as long as you two are together,
Have children and are married forever.
It is considered a sweet success,
In the eyes of your parents.

Silent Symphony

Unheard.
Whether you
Shriek, scream or shout.

Judge a Book

    remorse-   -er   -is   -and   -er   -ir.
A   -ful widow- ran h-   h-   through h-   ha-
   beauti-   -er   -unting knife   -is   -mstring.

Pain

In a time of pain,
No one is to be found,
But in a time of play,
Everyone comes right 'round.

Mourn

I mourn your absence
As if death himself has taken you.

When

I knew it was over
The moment
You disappeared from reality
And started appearing
Only in my dreams.

Red Sky

The way she painted
The skies red
Would make you think
She was an artist
In a past life.

Thorns

Her parents stood proudly
Watching their daughter grow,
For she was flourishing
Because they were ever so nourishing.
However, once they saw
Their beloved daughter
Wasn't a lovely daisy,
But rather a crimson rose,
They could not see past
Her tiny, little thorns,
And so, they had begun
To mourn,
Before they decided
To have her petals torn
In the hopes of
Making her reborn.
But instead, it just left her
Wishing she had been stillborn.

Heart

He loved until his heart
Could no more.

Stained Petals

I knew that everyone's time
Would come to an end.
After all, no one can stay
Here forever,
Whether it be near, there or anywhere.
But I never thought
Anything could take you
And your magnificent heart
That had the ability to thaw
The coldest of frostbites
And secure the very beams this house stood.
I always imagined you a part of my life.
As far as my eyes could see
You were immortal.
Nothing could touch you.
Everything was going remarkably well,
So why did it have to go so wrong?
I was supposed to make you proud today
By showing you the very campus
That would help me
Finally be able to give back to you.

Not to mention,
It was time for you to relax
And watch the seeds you planted.
But instead, it is now
Time for you to lie
Beneath the soil
With bloodstained petals
Laying on your chest.

Veins

I'm hurting
But feel no pain.
I've been long gone
With only blood still in my veins.

Soul

Why do I miss you so?
Is it because of the way
You caressed my soul?
Or perhaps the fact that
You had gone where the others
Couldn't bear to go,
Not only partaking
In this wild journey with me,
But begging, asking for more?

In Love

She frowns;
He smiles.

In love

She is;
He was.

Story of My Life

You were just a chapter,
Not the entire book.

CPSIA information can be obtained
at www.ICGtesting.com
Printed in the USA
BVHW040727121222
653961BV00003B/3